Nursery Rhymes
Hey, Diddle, Diddle

And Other Best-Loved Rhymes

ARCTURUS

This edition published in 2012 by Arcturus Publishing Limited
26/27 Bickels Yard, 151–153 Bermondsey Street,
London SE1 3HA

ISBN: 978-1-84858-678-9
CH002346US
Supplier 15, Date 0412, Print run 1754

Printed in China

Hey, Diddle, Diddle

Hey, diddle, diddle,
The cat and the fiddle,
The cow jumped over
the moon.

The little dog laughed,
To see such a sport,
And the dish ran away
with the spoon.

Rock-a-Bye, Baby

Rock-a-bye, baby,
In the tree top.
When the wind blows,
The cradle will rock.

When the bough breaks,
The cradle will fall.
Then down will come baby,
Cradle and all.

It's Raining, It's Pouring

It's raining, it's pouring,
The old man is snoring.
He went to bed,
And bumped his head,
And couldn't get up in the morning.

One, Two, Buckle My Shoe

One, two,
Buckle my shoe;
Three, four,
Knock at the door;
Five, six,
Pick up sticks;
Seven, eight,
Lay them straight;
Nine, ten,
A good, fat hen;

Eleven, twelve,
Dig and delve;
Thirteen, fourteen,
Maids a-courting;
Fifteen, sixteen,
Maids in the kitchen;
Seventeen, eighteen,
Maids a-waiting;
Nineteen, twenty,
My plate's empty!

Hush, Little Baby

Hush, little baby, don't say a word,
Papa's going to buy you a mockingbird.

And if that mockingbird won't sing,
Papa's going to buy you a diamond ring.

And if that diamond ring turns brass,
Papa's going to buy you a looking glass.

And if that looking glass gets broke,
Papa's going to buy you a billy goat.

And if that billy goat won't pull,
Papa's going to buy you a cart and bull.

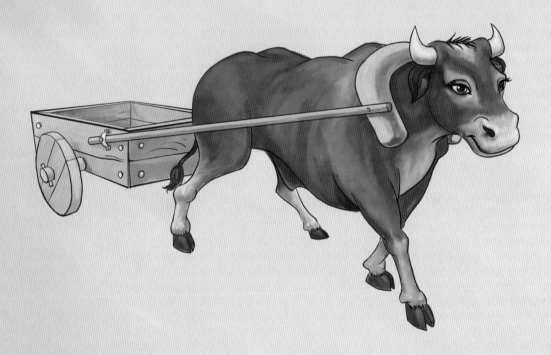

And if that cart and bull turn over,
Papa's going to buy you a dog named Rover.

And if that dog named Rover won't bark,
Papa's going to buy you a horse and cart.

And if that horse and cart fall down,
You'll still be the sweetest little baby in town.

Ding, Dong, Bell

Ding, dong, bell,
Kitty's in the well!
Who put her in?
Little Tommy Lin.
Who pulled her out?
Little Johnny Stout.

What a naughty boy was that
To try to drown poor kitty-cat.
Who never did him any harm,
But killed all the mice in his father's barn!

Eenie, Meenie, Minie, Moe

Eenie, Meenie, Minie, Moe,
Catch a tiger by the toe.
If he hollers, let him go,
Eenie, Meenie, Minie, Moe.